LIKE AN ASSASSIN

JONATHAN EVAN HUDSON

Copyright © 2025 by Jonathan Evan Hudson

All rights reserved.

No part of this book may be reproduced in any form or by any electronic or mechanical means, including information storage and retrieval systems, without written permission from the author, except for the use of brief quotations in a book review.

❀ Formatted with Vellum

LIKE AN ASSASSIN

CHAPTER
ONE

THE WORLD. Frozen still.

And upside-down?

Like the two-lane road several feet above Jake Walker. That dark asphalt rolled forward like a dead-tired dog's tongue—and just as smelly. As smelly as Poo Poo—his little corgi back home in his studio apartment.

So yeah, as smelly as the wind gusting against his back. Wind flapping his loose tee wildly—loose thanks to losing over fifteen pounds recently. Wind suddenly carrying the strong smell of freshly chewed strawberry gum.

Weird.

Weirder than how the clear blue sky was now below him. How his slip-on boots of dark-brown leather suddenly seemed so much heavier. Heavy toward the sky. Not the ground.

And now. Not a car in sight.

Not a single one parked along the concrete sidewalks along either side of the road. None.

Not another person either—despite a whole few blocks before the road ended at the twin oak doors of the pale-graystone chapel. Its upside-down steeples. More like a cluster of fangs. Stone fangs worthy of some kind of monster rabbit. Decorated here and there with little colorful panes of painted glass.

The dead center of the afternoon in downtown Fredericksburg ... Virginia. The state for lovers or something like that but no. Jake hadn't had a lover in decades—despite moving to the state a few years ago. Not since his childhood sweetheart and best friend rejected him for the football captain after their high school years together.

Never mind back then Jake was also voted least likely to ever have a James Bond lifestyle—a vote proved very wrong over the next decade. The stories he could tell ... and weren't allowed to ... still.

Why was he thinking of *that*? Everything upside-down and yet ...

Wait. The chapel. It should be **behind** Jake. Not in front.

And along the last block ... along both sides of the street. The line of colorful two-story townhouses. Townhouses built from wood as creaky old as the tales his grandma spun each and every Christmas. He just finished that block only a few several moments ago. Crossed the one-way road cutting across the two-laner.

Only moments ago ... what was Jake doing?

Oh yeah.

Walking down the sidewalk. A few feet ahead of him. A small pouch of a bookbag. Shiny neon red. Thin pink stretchy straps. Strapped tight to the back of some really lovely looking college girl. A gorgeously long-haired blonde college girl. Jogging briskly in a neon-pink two-piece sports bikini and glowingly-bright neon-pink sneakers.

Moments ago she had jogged passed him.

Just as a few sudden snaps. The bookbag fell off her. Tight straps had snapped—broken.

Yet his training from decades ago kicked in for some reason—and he caught the bookbag. Called out to the beautiful blonde college girl—who must not have heard him and kept jogging.

Until he dashed up to her and tapped her shoulder and ... ack!

Now. The world spun again. Spinning fast. So fast.

The sky. It spread wide. Blue. In front of him? What the ... the wind still gusted against his back.

Until—bang!

His back. The concrete sidewalk. Pain. Serious. Aching. Pain. Blood-in-mouth pain.

And a realization.

Someone had flipped him over. Quick and skillfully.

Least a soft slim arm saved his head—and only his head. Only for a moment too. Before it too slipped away. His head clunking against the ground. Not the first fall he suffered through and certainly not the last.

Least he didn't let go of the bookbag—even when his head clunked against the concrete.

And stars ... stars ... stars twinkling as much as a starry dark night—despite it being the middle of the bright and sunny afternoon. A steaming hot afternoon. The mugginess not helping one bit either.

The beautiful blonde college girl gasped. Still out of his sight.

"Oh. *My.* **Gawd**," she said. "I. am. SO sorry!"

From the bubbly sound of her candy-sweet voice she crouched close to but beyond his head and vision. Not that it mattered. It seemed like his head was swimming through sludge.

"Reflex," she said. "Sorry. Quick self-defense reflex. That's all. I ..."

More like assassin reflex. Damn was she skilled. As skilled as Jake used to be. As some of the better assassins for that secret society of crime and terror known as Manticore, or even the secret crime organization known as Mantis ... no. Not important. Not now.

This college girl was just another beautiful college girl.

That's all.

So whimpering Jake lifted her bookbag. The straps dangled down, on the sidewalk beside his chest.

Obviously the straps had snapped broken. Why ... who knew?

Why the bookbag was amazingly heavy ... like there was a weight or two in it, despite its small size so—with a wobbling grip—Jake managed to dangle the bookbag over himself, over toward the college girl.

"Lost ... bookbag ... delivery," Jake said. "To a Miss ..."

"Ooo!" the girl said. "Oops! Happened again. I really need to get a new bag but ... sigh,. I'm Petra and ..."

Suddenly a roller skater zoomed up to his other side. Passed his head.

But ... there hadn't been any sign of anyone else in either direction other than Petra—

"Yoink!"

CHAPTER
TWO

YOINK?

Spoken by another girl? Less bubbly voiced and far less candy-sweet voiced than the beautiful blonde Petra near Jake and his head.

Stars still filled his vision. His whole entire vision. The bright blue sky above him. It twinkled full of too many fake little dotty stars. The even brighter afternoon sun forced Jake to squint up rather than stare anywhere but no.

The store to his side. A wide white sign unreadable from this low close angle hung over the entrance.

Jake had been flipped in front of the entrance then.

The sign was framed by colorful light bulbs. None of which were on now. And a pair of square glass displays. Jake recognized those white silky lace dresses within the displays. Years, if not decades there and yet still as pricy as ever.

Even the smell.

Despite the freshly chewed strawberry gum from Petra. The stink of freshly laid asphalt.

Loads and loads of ancient clothing mustiness out did them completely here.

How ... a miracle in itself.

Kinda like how he survived so many missions to stop Manticore or other trouble.

The glass displays even formed a short hallway to the front door. A short hallway just wide enough to fit a cubby but tall person with their arms spread wide out. That hallway couldn't even be seen except when you were right in front of it. Like a secret hallway. Almost.

So that's where the roller skater must have hid. Least for a while.

Jake tried to glance toward that other girl. The roller skater.

But his aching body refused to budge. Yet. The concrete sidewalk. So scolding hot now. Frying hot now. His back. Like the best kind of French fries fried to the crispy death now.

Not exactly the best landing spot. Or bed. But alive was better than not.

(Usually.)

An instant later it happened.

That other girl. She snatched the bookbag from Jake. Ripping it out of his hand. Opposite side of Petra.

That deep zoom of her roller skates. She passed Petra an instant later.

"Hey!" Petra said. "No! No! No! Give that back! I **need** it!"

Uh huh. Jake's gone this far.

Time to push even further.

So clenching his teeth Jake arched his aching back. Ignoring the pain screaming at him he scanned the upside-down world behind him.

Just empty sidewalk? To the one-laner street and beyond. To the chapel.

No sign of the roller skating thief?

What in the ...

Just as a business card fluttered down. Right in front of his face.

A white business card. One with an all-too-familiar symbol—a golden circle with a barbed hook end on the top—like a toupee—and two big black triangular eyes.

The emblem of Manticore? Here?

What in the ...

CHAPTER
THREE

BACK ON HIS feet Jake had to admit to himself he was out
of training to say the least.

No matter how much his body still ached all over ... down
the concrete sidewalk—either direction and either side—not a
single sign of anyone. No one.

Only Jake and Petra here.

For the moment.

No doubt someone somewhere was watching them. From a
window. From a darkened store. Somewhere within the block.
Or where the whole entire block could be watched.

Manticore was like that. Exactly like that.

Sure a camera could be used but with generative AI nowadays the video could be faked all-too-easily as well.

Why the two-lane road was emptier than his bank account
before payday. Not that his data analyst job nowadays paid all
that well. Better than nothing—least until his art skills got
good enough to cover some bills. So a few more years at the
very least.

Never mind the stray one-way one-laners. They cut across the two-laner and made blocks at regular intervals.

All very much empty.

Strange.

Very strange.

Even for Manticore. Normally he'd get attacked by gang of thugs. Least by now.

The bells of chapel even started dinging their hourly jiggle. Reminding everyone within hearing range it was 1500, or 3 PM, the dead center of the afternoon here in downtown Fredericksburg, but weird how empty the area was.

Usually there was a little traffic. A stray person or two, at the very least.

Not completely and utterly empty. Even now. At the least busy time of the day.

No.

This place was almost as empty as nighttime. Dead center of nighttime on a weekday early in the week. The emptiest time ever, as Jake discovered back a couple of years ago, back when he needed to grab a late night snack and nothing was open, not even a late night convenience store.

Something was off ... but what?

Beside Jake poor Petra was on her knees, and damn, looking down at Petra ... well, from her big blue eyes down to her lightly tanned thighs, wow, compared to those gorgeous big-breasted blondes generated by AI found everywhere online, well, Petra had them all beat in every way possible, in the best ways possible.

Including the chest.

Gulp was awkwardly right.

Her two-piece sports bikini left almost nothing to the imagination either. That neon-pink spandex even seemed to glow as bright as her blue eyes. That her golden hair flowed straight down to the nap of her back. How her hair covered more of her than her spandex sports bikini ... along with those neon-pink running sneakers ...

A glance over the Manticore business card ... on its back ... the word "JOE" ...

A name? What the ... and then a dash and the name "Petra."

Jake slipped the Manticore business card into his right pocket. His shorts should be loose enough that it wouldn't be obvious that he had it in there.

"You know a Joe?" Jake said. "Or ..."

"Or what?" Petra said. "That bag. It had our rent money. Our grocery money. All of it. For the month. And now ... now ..."

She whimpered. Hugging herself. And cringing./

"How do I tell," Petra said, "gramps and the others? That I ... I ..."

"Let's get it back then," Jack said. "Or call the police ... up to you. I—"

"No police!" Petra said. "We'll ... we'll never get it back then. I know. Know that girl. She's already long gone. But ... I do have an idea ... an idear to catch her and more ... if you'll help me."

"Sure," Jake said. "Helping a damsel in distress ... I'm old fashioned in that way."

With an awkward giggle Petra smiled up at Jake. Her grin a brilliant white. Making Jake smile right back at her.

Even as she hopped up to her feet.

Grabbed his hand.

And led the way inside the entrance? Hurrying to the unknown.

THE DARK UNKNOWN least to Jake.

He never bothered to step inside this place. Not once in his few years here in Fredericksburg. Just the loads and loads of mustiness deterred him. Too much like his parent's attic. Including the old junk. Clearly this place was an antique store of some sort. And dark enough to hint-hint that it really wasn't open right now ...

Despite its squeaky glass door being completely unlocked.

Despite the squeaky door closing by itself with a loud bang.

Jake let Petra lead him. Hand holding hand. His heart thumping loud in his ears since wow, was Petra gorgeous, and amazingly hopeful for the situation at hand, for losing so much money.

Since at the moment towering high cabinets formed a canyon around them. A canyon of furnished brown wood. Complete with fancy brass knobs. Some even reminding Jake of his grandma's favorite cabinets with their kitty head style knobs.

Petra led Jake deeper and deeper into the dark silent store. Too silent.

Not even the stray bing or crack. As if no one else was here yet.

A glance at the ceiling. More wood planks. No sign of lightning—or anything to turn on and light the place.

Yet.

Only the squeak-squeak-squeak of Petra's sneakers against the floor of creaky wood planks. Planks that even sank a little with each of their steps. Not exactly a confidence builder but fitting with the old-fashioned decor here perfectly.

A few cabinets before the end of the canyon. Facing them. A few feet from the last of the cabinets. A towering high glass display. Shelves and glass shelves full of shiny nicely-painted porcelain figurines?

No need to see the price tags of those figurines to know those delicate-looking things were far from cheap. Enough to cost a good chunk of his biweekly pay—and his pay wasn't exactly half bad.

Not good but not bad either.

Kinda like what his amazing mentor, Halter the Hero, called Jake at his skill level.

Least back while he was in perfect shape—fighting and physically.

But before Petra reached the end of the towering high cabinets she turned to the second-to-last cabinet to the left. A cabinet similar to a closet. Twin doors high and wide enough to fit a jolly fat Santa. Their knobs—candy-cane style spirals?

Wow. Christmas in July? Nice.

But stranger and stranger too. But Manticore had weirdness in spades.

Usually.

Without a glance back at Jake Petra knocked the right door twice quickly. Then the left once.

Paused a moment. A silent tense moment.

Then she knocked the right door again twice. Quickly.

Then opened both doors at once and woh.

Not just a closet-style cabinet. Inside, on the bottom, an open trap door revealed a stairway down into the dark unknown. A stairway of concrete steps. Shallow steps leading into deep darkness.

No sign of whoever opened that trap door but ...

"Come on!" Petra said. "Don't chicken out now."

Jake nodded. Mouth drying. Heart thumping.

Since there was no missing the emblem of Manticore etched right over the stairway. That golden circle with a barbed hook on top. Its triangular black eyes. Despite the dim light. Despite the sinister air of it all. Despite the obvious danger here and beyond.

Jake wasn't even armed and yet ... no turning back now.

Trap or no.

"No worries," Jake said. "I love a good chicken but not *that* much. Let's go."

With a all-too-happy giggle Petra led Jake into the cabinet ... and down the dark concrete stairway.

Down into the dangerous unknown.

CHAPTER
FIVE

OUT OF ALL THE places Jake expected Petra to drag him down to—an underground fighting arena full of loud and rowdy betting?

No doubt what in this hidden basement was either.

Underneath that antique store Petra had flipped him over in front of. This basement. Exactly where the cabinet's concrete stairway led them to. A least a couple flights underground to the edge of this round room of unpainted concrete. Several dozen feet wide.

Just bright enough to kinda sortof see around but not by much.

(How this place was so well hidden ...)

No mistaking the strong smell of alcohol. Strong enough to get a guy drunk without sipping a drop. Too much like some of the better bars and night clubs in the area. But that was only after 10 PM or so. Never this early. Afternoon early.

(Never mind Petra definitely didn't look old enough to have any alcohol legally either.)

((Never mind how the big-bellied bouncer let her slip by with nothing more than a glance.))

(((And thanks to Petra tugging him along, Jake only received a silent glare.)))

The rowdy sweaty crowd cheered and jeered for the two musclebound hulks in shiny boxer shorts in that cage. A young but rough crowd. College and older high schooler, mostly, guessing by the loud ... commentary and the lack of beards and younger look of most of the crowd.

Despite the dim light that much was obvious.

Solid steel mesh balled over the canvas stage in the very center of the basement. The canvas stage was stained dark with plenty of blood. Old and new stains. Both hulks pommeled each other. Hulks not much older than Petra, probably, judging by their immature stubble and ruined baby faces. Each added plenty of blood to stain the canvas each and every moment.

Too much like the kind of fights Jake used to have—but not as dirty.

Not as life and death.

The warm concrete floor around the arena slanted downward. Descending several feet before reaching the stage. So the entire crowd had a decent view of the stage. A stage only a dozen or so feet wide.

Just big enough for serious one-on-one fights.

But yet both hulks fought in the very center. Neither giving an inch to the other. No one was flung against the steel cage mesh.

Yet.

Petra tugged Jake through the rowdy crowd. Shoving through and around the people without a hint of hesitation or mercy. Not a single apology give or taken. Just pure cocky you know. Since there was no missing the loads of acne over some of their young faces.

Even as they cheered and jeered for the hulks in the arena.

More than a few glanced her way. From muscular meat-head to scrawny nerd they all clearly strained themselves for the courage to do more than just glare, or ogle Petra, but no.

Her speed through the dense crowd gave none of them anywhere near enough time to build up the courage to do anything but glance her way and yearn to take Jake's place.

And Jake ... back in his high school and early college days ... he'd received the same kind of glances and glares from so-called friends.

Until his childhood sweetheart finally broke up with him.

Strange to think Petra was, might be like a second chance, in some weird odd way but ...

Petra suddenly stopped right next to the cage.

Right in front of some gangly guy in rough dark-blue jeans and no shirt. Even with both hands in his pockets that wiry wicked-looking goon had more stubble over his head and face than sense in those blood-shot eyes.

He couldn't be any older than twenty or so. Maybe younger. Maybe a lot younger.

But strong.

Too strong for Jake to fight hand-to-hand without a plan and win, let alone survive. Not unless Jake restarted his daily martial arts training routine once again.

And only after a few weeks, no, months of restarting his training.

Petra grimaced at the gangly goon. Several inches shorter than him, but showing not a drop of fear.

Good.

Those kind of guys preyed on anyone who foolishly showed them any fear.

"Hey! Vic!" Petra said. "Down here!"

"I see ya, bitch," Vic said. "You missed the last two fights."

"I know, I know," Petra said. "Cut me some slack and—"

"Slack?" Vic said. "Do I looked like a charity?"

"Of course not," Petra said. "But—"

"Shut up," Vic said, "since you didn't put up."

Petra huffed. Motioned at Jake beside her.

"This guy will pay my fee," Petra said, "in return for my winnings today."

"You got a sugar daddy now?" Vic said. "I make ten times that old dude does."

Old dude? Jake almost barked out a laugh but knew better.

Silence was sometimes stronger than even laughter.

Petra let out a sultry laugh. Rubbed her amazingly fine behind against Jake ... and his crotch and ... wow. Heart attack from utter bliss possible right about now.

Despite the utter bliss over his crotch Jake stayed utterly, utterly calm.

And simply raised a skeptical eyebrow at that annoying Vic.

"Immature guys are so ..." Petra said.

"Or so what?" Vic said. "Dump the loser and—"

"And what?" Petra said. "I lose the match and—"

"Your dud's toast," Vic said. "Unless ..."

"Fine, fine," Petra said. "I'll fuck your brains out instead ... if I lose—but when I win you pay up ten times the—"

"Ten?" Vic said, "You think I'm made of money now?"

Jake sighed. Shook his head in disappointment.

"Small talk. Small guy," Jake said. "Bragging about ten times the money and yet—"

Vic snarled at Jake. "Bitch! You stay out of this!"

Petra tsked. Leaning into Jake even more and Jake. He. He couldn't help but enjoy it too much.

Far too much.

"He's in," Petra said. "**All** in."

"His funeral then too," Vic said. "And one fuck won't cover your debt—when you lose, bitch."

"I know, I know," Petra said. "Since when have I lost? It's not like Amanda Roundhouse is even still—"

Vic smirked so suddenly wicked that ... Jake forced himself not to gulp.

"Oh Amanda just got back," Vic said. "Eager to kick your ass and make you **all** ours."

Petra merely pouted. The sudden nervous tension in her body obvious—and not just by touch.

"Amanda ... she ..." Petra said.

"Deal's a deal, bitch," Vic said. "I told you you'd regret ditching our first offer."

Offer? What kind of ... the crowd around the three of them ... not as close now. And getting further and further away. Giving the three of them space.

Too much space.

"I know, I know," Petra said. "Next match will settle it all ..."

That's when Vic said the utterly unexpected.

"Not just you, bitch," Vic said. "Petra, it's a tag team effort. You and your bitch. Against Amanda and Killjoy Jones. Time to die, bitches."

And the way Petra suddenly squeezed Jake's hand ... no escaping this mess unscathed.

Jake squeezed hers back just as tenderly. Hoping beyond hope that this wasn't some elaborate setup.

Hoping he wasn't another sucker Petra just lured to his doom.

Hoping he could somehow save Petra from this mess.

Not become the mess itself.

Just as a loud thump rang out—one o the hulks lay unmoving on the canvas stage.

A roar erupted and called out: "Killjoy Jones! Killjoy Jones! Killjoy Jones!"

On the bright side Killjoy Jones already had taken a beating.

On the dark side Killjoy hopped and cheered energetically. Already warmed up. Clearly not the least bit winded from the fight.

And more than ready for the next one.

The one against Petra and Jake.

CHAPTER
SIX

A LOUD METALLIC clink behind Jake and both Jake and Petra were trapped on the canvas stage. Already the light shined so bright it shut out the crowd beyond the cage. The crowd still jeered at the two of them. At Jake and Petra beside each other. Loud and rowdy as before.

Jake and Petra both stood, waiting ready a few feet from the edge of the steel cage. Far enough to avoid being grabbed by anyone from the crowd.

(Hopefully.)

The match before—how it ended. So suddenly. The crowd roaring its brutal approval.

The lights baked Jake like bowl of ice cream trapped in an oven. His tee and shorts were too loose for the fight. They could easily be grabbed. Just like Petra and her long blonde hair could be grabbed and no.

Like Halter the Hero drilled into Jake years ago—don't focus on your own disadvantages.

Focus on overcoming them. Overcoming the problems ahead.

Not on the problems themselves.

Too bad there was no chance to change into something more ... suited for the coming fight. Not even a pair of gloves. For either Jake or Petra. Let alone warm up for the coming beating.

Several feet across from them. On the stage. The surviving hulk of towering brawn known as Killjoy Jones. Still in those shiny boxers and nothing else. Hands wrapped in rough-looking blood-soaked fabric. Only feet in front of Jake.

Beside Jones was a gangly girl with short dark hair and a sneer as wretched as her wicked pair of brass knuckles.

Amanda what's-her-face, then.

Jake. His back. It still ached from Petra flipping him earlier but not enough to stop him—or worry him.

Much.

So, of course, Jake let the ache help him pretend to shirk, to look intimidated by Jones. Best get underestimated. Take advantage of their overconfidence. Attack suddenly and over-whelmingly.

A metallic clank-clank-clank rang out above them. Above the steel cage.

(The bell to start the fight?)

Both Jones and Amanda charged forward. Before the bell started ringing.

Pounding the canvas stage like they were about to pound Jake and Petra.

Only an instant to react.

To counter their coming doom.

But their fate—it seemed sealed.

Until Jake lunged forward. Suddenly.

Leaping high and fast.

Roaring his lungs out.

Slowing Jones down a touch.

Just like so many times in the past. Back when Jake fought Manticore. Death matches and worse.

Jones then gasped. Unable to completely stop his charge.

React in time.

Even when Jake crashed into Jones. His chest crashing into Jones' face. Arms wrapping around, strangling the hulk's thick neck.

Jake and his own body. His own weight. Enough to jolt Jones backwards.

Stumble backwards.

Faster and faster.

Until bang!

Jones smashed into the steel cage. Smashing Jake in the face too. Steel mesh to his face.

But Jake wasn't done.

Everything or nothing. Better take Jones down now or never. No chance Jones would underestimate Jake again. No.

So despite the pain. The agony. His breath. Held. Tense.

Jake dropped.

Using the cage for leverage. Despite the agony through his arms.

Shoved all his weight down. Down onto Jones' feet. Heels solidly onto toes.

Crunching them against the canvas stage.

Jones shrieked. Too shocked to counter Jake. Jake and his next move.

Jake rolled backwards. Pulling Jones down with him. Rolling him over.

Flipping Jones.

Despite the hulk's massive size. Weight. And strength.

Boom!

Jones was down. On his back.

And completely out.

Just as another shriek rang out. To the right of Jake—Petra stumbled backwards. Clutching her gut.

Till she crashed into the steel cage.

Amanda what's-her-face. Her back. To Jake.

So Jake. He lunged at Amanda. Tackling her at knee level. Tumbling her down like a wobbly tree blown down by a strong wind.

Her yelp.

Bang to the ground a moment later.

The silence. From the crowd.

Deafening.

Too deafening. Something worse was about to happen.

And moments later—it did.

CHAPTER
SEVEN

VICTORY WAS THEIRS—OR so Jake had hoped.

The jeering crowd. Finally silenced.

The blinding lights—still too bright to see beyond the steel cage. Too much like the headlights of an incoming car at night. Still as roasting hot as ever. Hotter than Petra in her two-piece sports bikini in fact.

Jones moaned on the canvas stage to Jake's left.

Amanda groaned on the stage to his right.

Several feet away The stage cage ... Petra beamed at Jake.

Except Vic and the big-bellied bouncer were already inside the cage. Vic was behind Petra. Holding a gleaming steel switchblade to her throat. His other arm tight around her waist. Her hands gripped the thug's forearm but no use.

How'd that Vic sneak up on Petra? Just grabbing her shoulder before got Jake flipped.

Unless ...

Vic snarled. "Beat that bitch down!"

"Righto Boss," the big-bellied bouncer said.

Brass knuckles now on his thick hands. The bouncer

loomed closer and closer to Jake. Jake edged back more and more.

Vic growled. "This is your fault, Petra! Join or else! Else that dud dies here and now!"

What ... Join or else ... Joe ...

"Don't worry about me," Jake said. "My luck's hadn't run out—yet."

"Oh yet?" the bouncer said. "Luck's run out, bitch."

Except it hadn't.

Petra—like an assassin—suddenly flipped Vic over—and right smack into the back of the bouncer.

Toppling them both over. Both landing with a loud thump. Crashing in a pile. Struggling and moaning.

Petra barked a laugh. "Who's the bitch now, bitches!"

The crowd roared its approval now? Fickle crowd but at least—

"FREEZE!" A commanding voice shouted. "POLICE!"

CHAPTER EIGHT

BACK ABOVE GROUND and in front of the antique store once again. This time Jake was right-side up on the sidewalk, not flat on his back, and far less achy as he stood there, rearing to head back home to his studio apartment.

Back to his corgi and an early dinner of roasted chicken and potatoes.

Even if the sun seemed even hotter than before. Roasting hot despite a few clouds in the sky now. Hotter than the evening he had hoped to spend with Petra tonight. Well.

After he cleared up this stunningly amazing mess.

Since now red-and-blue lights of the police flashed everywhere along the street. Sirens wailed here and there. Loud enough to drown out his thoughts for a few moments. Especially his heart pounding in his ears.

But not the relief of being alive and well once again.

Jake rubbed his wrists. The cuffs already off. Since, of course, perk of his heroic past coming to help—according to several of the officers now leading countless cuffed goons into police vans. Their curses and fury now useless.

Apparently this had been a long-awaited bust on Manticore but ...

Petra was now cuffed too. Being led to the police car beside Jake. Head down in utter shame.

Jake tried to speak with the big-shouldered detective leading Petra to the car. A few waves of the hand and Jake managed to get his attention but the detective simply shook his head.

"Count yourself lucky, Jake," the detective said. "Everyone else here's going to do some serious time for their involvement in Manticore. Even the girl. We've got plenty of evidence. So ... just say your good-byes quickly. Best not get too involved anymore."

Jake sighed. He already was involved and ... time for a little miracle.

Hopefully.

So he reached into his pocket. Handed over the business card to the detective.

"Join Or Else, Petra," Jake said. "That's what it means. They were trying to recruit her—she hadn't joined them so—"

The detective tsked. "It's ... a stretch but ..."

"Some roller skater thief," Jake said, "Stole her bookbag and all her money for the month. We were trying to recover it. That's all. That thief—"

"Amanda Roundhouse," the detective said. "we recovered the bookbag and everything in it but the evidence inside ..."

The detective shook his head.

Petra still hung her head too low to even meet Jake's eyes.

"Other evidence?" Jake said. "But ..."

Then an old familiar voice barked a gruff huff behind Jake —Halter the Hero? Here?!

"But what?" Halter said. "You think my granddaughter—"

Jake and the detective gasped together. "Granddaughter?!"

Moments later Petra was freed, and after a quick thankful and final wonderful hug with Jake, Petra headed away, down the sidewalk, alongside with her hulk of a leathery grandfather.

With a dejected sigh Jake turned, and headed back himself. The chapel bells rang loud and all too heart-achingly clear. So he slipped his hand into his pocket for his phone to call ... huh?

A business card instead?

Yeah.

A business card with an address for a local dojo. But on the other side ... another address a good several blocks away from the dojo. Written in pink pen. A time later tonight.

And a two very cutesy pink hearts around the name Petra.

How she managed this card ... when ... damn. She was Halter's granddaughter alright.

Like an assassin—but sweeter.

WANT MORE?

Go to
www.JonathanEvanHudson.com

www.ingramcontent.com/pod-product-compliance
Lightning Source LLC
Chambersburg PA
CBHW011153190726
48288CB00010B/3300